Dedicated to my uncle, George Blechta, with
great fondness and with gratitude for his help
and support over the years.

CHAPTER ONE

Pratt felt like pounding his head on his desk. Why couldn't McDonnell just leave him alone today?

He felt every one of his fifty-four years as he walked past all the empty desks to the office of the man who ran the Homicide Division. His desk was as far away from the office as he could get it.

"What can I do for you?" Pratt asked.

Captain McDonnell looked up from the papers on his desk. "There's a problem at Symphony Hall. A big problem."

"What?"

"I've just had a call from upstairs. Appears someone's murdered the damn conductor."

"Luigi Spadafini?"

"Yes—if he's the conductor. I thought it would be right up your alley. You like this kind of music so much."

"Thanks," Pratt answered glumly.

What he wanted at the moment was a good nap, not another job. The previous night he'd been wrapping up a tricky case and got exactly three hours' sleep on a sofa in an empty office he'd found. He had the stiff neck to prove it too.

"The chief wants you to tread lightly. That's the other reason I'm sending you. You know how to act around the symphony set."

"Anything else?"

McDonnell shook his head. "Nope. Just hustle down there. Once the press gets hold of the news, all hell's going to break loose."

As Pratt turned to go, his boss added, "Take Ellis with you. Show him the ropes. This promises to be a little out of the ordinary."

Just great. Saddled with the greenest member of the squad. Pratt didn't even know the kid's first name and didn't care to. Hopefully the young pup wouldn't screw anything up.

As he went back to his desk, the captain called, "Good job last night, Pratt. You did us proud."

Pratt bit his tongue. Then why not let someone else handle this job and let him go home?

Pratt let Ellis drive across town to the city's latest municipal wonder. Built four years earlier to a lot of taxpayer squawking, Symphony Hall was beautiful outside but cold and sterile. Inside, though, it was all wood, and the sound quality was lovely. He'd heard Beethoven's Fifth Symphony there the previous month, and it had been a concert he'd remember for a long time. Spadafini had been very impressive.

Now Pratt's head felt as if it was stuffed with sawdust. Great way to begin an investigation.

Ellis was a good-looking lad. Tall and still lanky, a lot like Pratt when he'd been that age. Thirty years later, he'd lost most of his hair and put on a good fifty pounds. At least he didn't need glasses—yet.

Making conversation, he asked, "How long have you been in Homicide?

"Two weeks, sir," Ellis answered.

"Seen any action yet?"

"Only that domestic murder last Friday. Terrible situation. Mostly I've been pushing papers."

"So I heard."

"I wanted to say that it's an honor to be working with you."

"I don't need buttering up, Ellis. You're here to make my life easier. Keep your eyes and ears open and try to stay out of my way."

"My pleasure, sir."

"And another thing: stop calling me 'sir.' Pratt will do."

The coast was still clear as they pulled up at the backstage entrance. Surprisingly, the media hadn't arrived yet. A beat cop Pratt recognized was standing next to the door, looking bored.

"Glad to have you aboard, sir," he said. "It's a madhouse in there, I hear."

"It's going to be a madhouse out here too. Don't let anyone in, and don't tell them anything."

"Right."

Later on Pratt was sorry that he had just rushed by. He might have retired on the spot if he'd known about the unholy mess he was walking into.

At the vacant security desk just inside, a sergeant Pratt knew was waiting.

Next to him stood a man wearing a suit and tie, even though it was Saturday morning. He looked to be in his late thirties, medium height, slightly overweight.

"Glad they sent you, Pratt," the sergeant said as they shook hands. "This is Michael Browne. He's the symphony's manager. He's the one who called the murder in."

Pratt knew Browne had to be competent to have this sort of job. At the moment, he looked pretty rattled and on edge.

More handshaking as Pratt introduced Ellis.

"The situation is a real mess," the sergeant added.

"Blood?" the detective asked. He hated the bloody ones.

"No, no. It's the suspect list."

"What about it?"

"The entire orchestra has confessed."

CHAPTER TWO

Ellis's jaw dropped.

Pratt kept his face expressionless. "Tell me about it," he sighed.

The sergeant flipped open his notebook. "The call came in at ten seventeen, and the nearest squad car was sent over. At ten twenty-six, they called for backup and I was dispatched with two additional men."

"Let's get another half-dozen down here. Make a perimeter at either end of the street outside to keep the media away. They'll be all over this place like a bunch of cockroaches. I want this building wrapped in crime-scene tape."

"I'll see to it."

"So when you got here, what did you find?"

"The body of the conductor in his office, and the orchestra waiting impatiently in the rehearsal room in the basement."

"How did they find out what had happened?"

Browne cleared his throat. "That was me, I'm afraid. I guess I was more shaken up than I thought. I just sort of blurted it out. Spadafini was our leader."

Pratt turned to him. "And their response?"

"Why, complete shock, of course. Who wouldn't have been shocked?"

Now to the heart of the matter. "And this mass confession, how did that come about?"

The sergeant took over again. "I told two of my officers to stay in the room with the orchestra and not let anyone leave. But there was no way to separate that many people to keep them from talking. I guess that's when they cooked this up."

Both police veterans knew the ploy was a dodge to protect the real killer—and that was a strange thing to do. There was more to this than met the eye.

Ellis looked as if he wanted to speak, so Pratt nodded to him.

"How many people are we talking about?" the young detective asked.

Browne cleared his throat. "Seventy-six."

Ellis whistled.

Pratt's frown deepened. "Who else is in the building today?"

"Just me," Browne said. When Pratt raised his eyebrows, the orchestra manager continued. "Four stagehands were here at the start of the rehearsal, but there was, um, a problem with Spadafini. They called what they refer to as a 'study session.'"

"Meaning they're off somewhere having coffee while they wait for the union rep to appear."

"Yes."

Pratt noticed that Ellis had his book out, taking notes. Either someone had told him about Pratt, or he was smarter than he looked.

"Cause of the friction?"

It was Browne's turn to sigh. "It's no secret that Spadafini could be quite difficult."

"But you're certain the stagehands were out of the building?"

"Yes. Shortly after the rehearsal began. I let them out myself. I was hoping to calm them down."

Pratt needed time to think. He knew he didn't have that time.

"I'd better see the body." He'd only taken two steps when he turned back to the sergeant. "I don't suppose there's any security surveillance of the murder scene? No?

Well, check whatever security footage there is for anything useful."

The conductor's office was one floor above. The door was slightly open. Since the Scene of Crime team hadn't yet arrived, Pratt took a package containing a pair of latex slip-ons from his coat pocket. He quickly snapped them over his shoes.

"Wait out here," he told Browne and Ellis.

Spadafini's body lay near the huge window behind his desk. Sadly, the building was covered in mirrored glass, so no one could have seen in. Pratt stood for nearly a minute, memorizing every detail in front of him. Then he moved toward the facedown body.

Thick wire was wrapped around the conductor's neck, which was heavily bruised. Fastened to each end of the wire were strange-looking drumsticks. "Do you know what this is around his neck?" Pratt yelled to Browne.

"I, ah, didn't take a close look. I just saw the maestro, ran to my office, picked up the phone and called the police."

"Sir, I mean, Pratt," Ellis asked, "do you mind if I have a look?"

"Do you have something for your feet?"

"Of course."

The youngster was soon standing next to him. "That looks like a cello string, and those sticks are definitely timpani mallets."

"How do you know?"

"I played trombone all through high school."

Pratt remained in the room for several more minutes, then went back out to the hall to wait for the arrival of the Scene of Crime team.

Pulling out his notebook, he turned to Browne. "Could you tell me your whereabouts in the building this morning?"

Browne's eyes opened wide. "You suspect me?"

"I suspect everyone and no one," Pratt answered, quoting Sherlock Holmes. Browne didn't seem to notice. "Just answer the question, please."

The other man looked up at the ceiling. "Well, I got here well before anyone arrived. I knew it was not going to be an 'easy' rehearsal. Everyone was pretty angry. I was present in the rehearsal room when the orchestra arrived. Of course, I had to deal with the stage-crew problem around that time."

"When was that?"

"Shortly after the rehearsal began. I talked to them for about fifteen minutes before they stormed out. Then I went up to my office to do some work."

"Is that near this office?"

Browne pointed. "Just down the hall, there."

"And you didn't hear anything?"

"I heard him storm down the hall at the beginning of the break. He was muttering to himself in Italian."

"Then what?"

"Well, I was on the phone to our secretary, looking for a package she was supposed to send out by courier yesterday. The person it was sent to hadn't received it yet, so I called her to ask what had happened."

"And?"

"She said she'd left it at the security desk. I went down to see if for some reason it was still there. When I came back up, I noticed Spadafini's door was open. When I looked in, I could see him lying on the floor behind his desk. I called the police immediately." He shivered. "I had to have just missed the murderer. I was gone barely five minutes."

Finally the elevator doors at the end of the hall opened, and the Scene of Crime team stepped out.

"I want a complete workup on this as soon as you can," Pratt told them. "I need to know what happened in a big hurry. They're leaning on me downtown." To Ellis he said, "Call the captain. Tell him I need every detective down here that he can spare—unless he wants us to bring an entire orchestra to him for questioning." Then he turned to Browne. "Don't leave the building. I will need to talk to you again later. Now could you show me where the orchestra is?"

"We should take the elevator down. It's faster."

As they descended to the basement and his first glimpse of the orchestra of self-confessed murderers, Pratt knew he was in for it.

CHAPTER THREE

P ratt walked through a set of double doors and into a large room.

Spread out in front of him should have been one of the country's great orchestras. On the podium should have been one of the best young conductors in the world. Great music should have been filling the space.

Instead people were spread about the room, talking in small groups. Seventy-six pairs of eyes looked up at the detective. He knew he needed to look deeply into all of them at the same time. That first glance often tells so much, and this time the opportunity was being wasted. Somewhere in this room was the person who knew exactly what had happened two floors above. Someone in this room had committed a cold-blooded murder.

He needed to say something—but what?

The two uniformed policemen stationed in the room, one male, one female, walked over to him.

"What's up?" the male asked in a low voice. "They're getting antsy."

"Have you kept them from using their cell phones?" Pratt asked, ignoring the question.

"Of course," the female officer answered, "but it's been hard."

"They don't want to listen to what we're telling them," the other added.

Pratt felt like telling them, "Of course! They're musicians." He refrained. At this point he needed all the help he could get. "Other than staging the largest mass confession ever, has anyone offered further information?"

"No—except for permission to use the restroom."

"Has anything happened that I should know about?"

"We were told to keep them here, accompany anyone who wanted to use the restroom, and keep our mouths shut. We've done that. As for anything suspicious, well, no."

Pratt nodded. "Fair enough. I'm going to talk to them, and there are too many for me to watch at once. While I speak, one of you watch the left-hand side of the group and the other the right. I want to know anything odd you see. Can I count on you? Good."

He walked over to the conductor's podium and stepped up. It seemed like the best place to make a speech. "Ladies and gentlemen, may I have your attention?"

Being disciplined musicians, all chatter stopped immediately. Several moved to their regular seats and sat.

"I am Detective Pratt and—"

"When are we going to be able to leave?" someone called out. "I have students this afternoon."

"When is someone going to tell us what's going on?" said a voice from the back.

Pratt put his hands up. "I only just arrived. Surely you understand how serious this matter is." Then he stopped and fixed them with a stare. "And just how seriously your behavior is being taken."

"What do you mean?" a younger man near the front asked.

"I know you're doing this to protect the murderer. It won't work. We will find out who did this. My best suggestion is for that person to come forward now. Then the rest of you can go home."

Pratt really didn't expect someone to just leap to their feet—but it would have been nice.

CHAPTER FOUR

As he spoke and answered the few questions he could, Pratt's eyes never stopped moving. The killer was somewhere in the room, and a telltale glance just might give him or her away. But there was nothing.

Browne, who had accompanied him from upstairs, picked up the dead conductor's overcoat, which had fallen off the back of his chair.

Pratt was momentarily distracted. "Put that down, please."

"Detective?"

His head turned right, where the cello section sat. An older woman had spoken. Rail thin with gray hair, she reminded Pratt of one of his grade-school teachers.

"Yes?"

She got to her feet. "I'd like to speak with you."

Pratt noticed that every eye in the room had turned to the woman. Not all were friendly.

It was best to keep his response as short as possible. "Yes, certainly. Would you come with me, please?"

Leaving the rehearsal room, the detective realized he didn't know where to take this woman. So he asked her to suggest someplace.

"I suppose the Green Room or one of the artists' dressing rooms." She strode through a doorway and up the stairs, forcing Pratt to keep up. "You'll need my name."

"Yes."

"Eliza Wanamaker."

Pratt realized this interview would be difficult. The woman was a "force of nature." This is what he called people who were hard to control and direct when being questioned.

Arriving at stage level, Eliza gestured left and right. "Green Room or dressing room?"

"What's a Green Room?"

She looked at him with pity. "It's the room where everyone waits before going on stage. And before you ask, it's very seldom actually painted green."

It was just to the right, bright and airy with large windows overlooking the loading dock for the stage. Sofas and chairs dotted the room, but they took their seats near the door.

The Wanamaker woman began speaking before Pratt could dig his note-book out of his inside jacket pocket.

"The first thing you must understand is that Luigi Spadafini was a first-class shit."

Pratt couldn't help blinking at the unexpected comment. "Pardon me?"

"There's no doubt about his musical gifts. The man was a bloody genius with a baton. But as a person, he deserved to die."

She sat back, crossing her arms. Her expression clearly dared Pratt to disagree.

"You're confessing?"

Eliza Wanamaker's guffaw filled the room. "Heavens no! I just thought you should know how the orchestra feels about our late conductor." She leaned forward again. "For months we've entertained ourselves with increasingly ridiculous ways to do him in."

"Sort of as a way to break the tension?"

She blinked in a surprised way. "Why, yes. I just never thought anyone would actually do it."

"But you do have some suspicions?"

"No idea."

"I find that hard to believe."

"Well, obviously, it had to be one of us."

"All of you felt that way?"

Disgust crossed Eliza's face. "There are always a few ass-kissers."

Pratt decided to switch channels. "You've made a pretty damning statement about Spadafini. Care to say more?"

Her face went hard. "Got a few hours?"

"Frankly, no. But I need some idea of what you mean."

"Tell me, Detective, have you ever even heard an orchestra play?"

Wanamaker's tone of voice made it clear she thought cops weren't capable of understanding classical music.

"I get to a half dozen of your concerts a year—when work doesn't get in the way. And I also enjoy opera. You really need to widen your views about the police."

She smiled for the first time. "Touché!"

"Now tell me what you know—or guess."

"Many of us hold Spadafini responsible for two deaths that have occurred in the orchestra since he took over."

"Two deaths?" Pratt got his pen busy in the notebook.

"Yes, last year, in a vendetta none of us understood, Spadafini rode our timpanist, Mort Schulman, until he had a heart attack from the stress."

"And you blame your conductor for this?"

"You weren't there! Everything Morty did was wrong. Spadafini took every opportunity to belittle him, to question his musical ability. Morty was only two years away from retiring. If it was so damned important, why didn't they just give him some money and let him go early?"

"And the other death?"

"Annabelle Lee, one of our cellists. She jumped in front of a subway train four months ago."

"Just how was Spadafini connected with this?"

"Everyone knew he was screwing her."

Pratt had heard of the unfortunate death. Every witness, and there were many, stated she had been alone at the end of the platform and clearly jumped. There had been no suicide note that he'd heard about.

"Really. You have proof of this?"

"It stands to reason. Within a week of a new piccolo player joining the orchestra, Annabelle was dropped, humiliated in front of the orchestra, and Spadafini was off pursuing his next conquest."

"Was he successful?"

Eliza Wanamaker glared at Pratt. "Why don't you ask the little fool yourself?"

CHAPTER FIVE

P ratt was interrupted by a knock on the door behind him. It was the sergeant from upstairs.

"Sorry to bother you. Five more detectives have arrived. You're also to call the captain right away. And the media have shown up—in force."

Pratt's sigh was heavy. "Where's young Ellis?"

"No idea."

"Find him. Send the detectives along to the rehearsal room. And get me Browne."

The sergeant started to turn away, then stopped. "Almost forgot. Someone sent these over. The captain wants everyone to carry one." He handed Pratt a walkie-talkie. "They're digital and encoded so the press can't listen in."

By the time Pratt got back to the rehearsal room himself, the detectives were coming down the hall. He outlined the situation as quickly as he could. The looks they passed among themselves told the story. They could see the mess they'd been dragged into.

Browne arrived, and Pratt asked him to arrange for each detective to have his own room to work in. By the time that was sorted out, they were down to storage rooms and even a broom closet.

Pratt addressed the newcomers. "This is all preliminary questioning. Just ask general questions. I want to know where everyone says they were during the break when Spadafini was murdered. Then we can cross-check that. I want your impressions of how truthful they're being. Make note of anything interesting. And above all, be quick. The press hounds are baying outside, and the whole city is watching."

"More like the whole world," one detective muttered.

Several of the detectives were shaking their heads as they went into the rehearsal room to get the first group of musicians for questioning.

Pratt pulled out his cell phone. He hated the damned things. But they were a fact of life for detectives these days, same as computers—which Pratt also hated.

Surprisingly, the captain picked up on the first ring. "What's the story, Pratt?"

"It's a total mess down here."

"Tell me something I don't know. Any progress?"

"Some," Pratt answered and gave his boss a quick update.

"I just got off the phone with the chief. The mayor's in his office, along with one of the symphony board's big shots. The chief stressed how they all wanted this situation resolved quickly."

Pratt rolled his eyes and felt a headache coming on. "The men just arrived, and I've given them their marching orders. The Scene of Crime team is also at work. We're moving as fast as we can."

"I'm counting on you, Pratt. Keep me in the loop. Understand?"

Captain McDonnell hung up before Pratt could even answer.

Ellis came hurrying down the hall. "I hear you wanted to speak to me."

"What have you been up to?"

"I was just talking to one of the Scene of Crime guys."

"And?"

"They're not coming up with much. There are no fingerprints on the murder weapon.

They doubt if they're going to get any DNA evidence, since the murderer was likely wearing gloves." Ellis took out his notebook and read. "Preliminary findings are that Luigi Spadafini was knocked to the ground and strangled from behind. The murderer had his—"

"Or her," Pratt interrupted. "Don't forget that an active woman could have done it. Spadafini was not a big man."

"Right. The murderer had his or her knee in the center of the conductor's back and pulled upward.

"Was the murderer left- or right-handed?"

"What?"

"A joke, Ellis. I was making a joke."

"Oh."

"Now I have a question for you. You said that string used to strangle Spadafini was from a cello. Are you sure?"

"It's too long for a violin or viola string and too short to come from a bass."

"And you know that from your high school music class."

"Yessir. My sister played the cello."

"You also said those sticks were used for playing the timpani. Again, certain?"

"Ninety-five percent." Ellis hesitated. "Why are you asking this?"

"I just had a very interesting conversation with a member of the orchestra. I do believe the murderer was trying to tell us something—or, more likely, muddy the trail." Pratt put his arm over Ellis's shoulder. "You had a satchel in the back of the car when we drove over. Am I right in thinking it contains a laptop computer?"

"Yes, it does."

"I'll bet a young buck like you is pretty good with them."

"They say I am."

"Can you do a little research for me?"

"Like what?"

"I've got two names: Mort Schulman, who played timpani for the orchestra, and Annabelle Lee, who played cello. They're both dead. Find out everything you can about them. Okay?"

Ellis's face brightened. "Sure. I'll get my laptop and go online as soon as I can find a place to sit down."

Pratt looked at Ellis. "Spare me the technical mumbo-jumbo. Just get me the information." As Ellis took off, Pratt called after him. "And I need it yesterday! Got that?"

The young detective waved over his shoulder as he crashed through the door at the end of the hall.

CHAPTER SIX

F inding himself alone for a moment, Pratt stepped into a nearby men's room to mentally catch his breath. He'd barely been here an hour, and so far he'd just been responding to the situation. The chance for the success of this investigation hung on whether he could begin to direct where things were going. He knew he would take the fall if this investigation went south.

At one of the sinks, he splashed several handfuls of water onto his face, enjoying the way it refreshed him. Looking at his reflection in the mirror as he turned off the water, Pratt felt depressed. He was developing jowls, the top of his head was shiny rather than covered with thick hair as it had been, and frankly, he looked terrible. Somehow his life was still on hold since his wife walked out on him over two years earlier.

Out in the hall again, he saw Browne leave the rehearsal room with the detectives and the first group of orchestra members to be questioned.

Pratt fell into step next to him. "I want to ask you a few questions."

"Certainly. I want to do anything I can to help in this crisis."

"Tell me what you know about Mort Schulman and Annabelle Lee."

"Tragic, both of them. Mort had frankly been getting old, and he was definitely overweight, but it was a shock to us all when he suffered his heart attack right after a concert."

"I heard Spadafini had been riding him for several months. Did he have something against Schulman?"

"That's news to me. Actually, I don't attend rehearsals all that much. My job also includes working with the conductor, guest artists, hall staff and, of course, the board members. All I know is, Mort didn't complain to me about Spadafini."

"And Annabelle Lee?"

"A lovely girl and one of our best young talents. Her passing was such a loss."

"Cut the public relations crap," Pratt growled. "I've got better things to do with my time."

Browne didn't answer. He showed each of the detectives the rooms they'd be using. Pratt waited, arms folded.

"All right, Detective Pratt," Browne finally said. "My job is to help keep this orchestra running smoothly. Spadafini's murder is a complete disaster for us.

I'm just trying to keep things going and minimize the fallout."

Pratt bit back a sharp answer that it was a greater tragedy for Spadafini. "So tell me about the two of them."

Browne sighed and looked down a moment. "There were rumors about Luigi and Annabelle—"

"I've heard it was more than rumors."

"All right! They were having an affair."

"Did Spadafini have a wife?"

"No. He said it would have cramped his Italian playboy lifestyle."

"Was there anyone else in the orchestra Spadafini was involved with?"

Browne sighed again. "Our new piccolo player."

"Was that recent?"

The orchestra manager looked uncomfortable. "I've heard through the grapevine that this is what upset Annabelle so much."

"Could it have driven her to suicide?"

"I...I don't know. Perhaps."

"I have one of my men checking on it, but you could help a lot if you'd tell me whether she left a suicide note."

"Look, Detective, this would have been a huge scandal if it had come out."

"Did she leave a suicide note?" Pratt repeated.

Even though they were alone in the corridor, Browne looked around before speaking. "I asked the maestro about it. He said there was a letter sent to his apartment. He told me he burned it without reading it."

"Did you believe him?"

Browne sighed. "Would you have wanted to read something like that?"

"And he or you never contacted the police." Pratt made it sound like a statement.

"There didn't seem to be any point. The girl obviously jumped in front of the train on her own. Fifty people must have seen it."

"Your conductor sounds like a heartless bastard."

"He could be." Browne looked away for a moment. "But he was a sublime musician."

"That doesn't excuse anything. You should have gone to the police with what you knew."

"What good would it have done? It's not as if Spadafini killed her himself."

Pratt fixed the manager with a hard stare. "It sounds to me like you're trying to excuse his behavior."

"He ran his life by a different set of rules than normal people. If you want to know, he told me that Annabelle became demanding. She wanted to move in with him, regularize their relationship. She didn't understand when he told her that this would never happen. He said he'd never led her on, made promises he didn't plan to keep."

"And you believe he was telling the truth?"

"How should I know? I wasn't his priest!"

At the end of the corridor, the door opened and one of the uniformed cops came through it.

"Detective Pratt?"

"What is it?"

"The orchestra is getting hungry."

Pratt looked at his watch: nearly twelve thirty. "I suppose we have to do something. They're going to be here a while longer—unless someone confesses."

Browne looked relieved as he said, "Occasionally, we have sandwiches brought in for long rehearsals. I'll see to it."

"One other thing, Browne. I need a list of all the orchestra members who are here today."

"I'll go up to my office and print it out."

As he hustled off, the uniform said, "You asked me to tell you if we spotted anything interesting. There's one woman who's been sitting in the back. She seems more upset than most of the others. People keep going back to talk to her."

"Let me guess: she's the piccolo player."

"What's a piccolo?"

As the two men headed back to the rehearsal room, Pratt was thinking to himself, This is going to be a very long day.

CHAPTER SEVEN

"Is there anything you'd like to tell me?" Pratt asked the short and very pretty young blond woman sitting in front of him. "I'm willing to hazard a guess that you play the piccolo," he added.

He'd asked the uniformed cop to send the upset woman out to speak to him. Once she'd appeared, Pratt had taken her upstairs and found the backstage area where he knew they could talk without being disturbed. This needed to be handled just right.

She sat stiffly with her hands clenched in her lap. "Actually, I play piccolo and flute in the orchestra."

Pratt pulled up another chair. "Your name, dear?"

"Sofia. Sofia Barna."

"That's Polish, isn't it?"

"My parents are from Poland. I was born in Toronto."

"And you've been in the orchestra how long?"

"Nearly six months."

"How do you like it here?"

"It's okay. I'm lucky to have landed the job."

"How are you finding life in our city?"

"All right, I guess."

Pratt circled a bit closer with the next question. "And when was the last time you saw Luigi Spadafini?"

Her eyes opened wide. "Why are you asking that?"

"Please answer the question."

Sofia looked around as if she wanted to run away.

"Take your time," Pratt said kindly.

"This morning just before he...just before he..."

Pratt studied her closely. Obviously she'd been crying, and right now her face looked like she just might do it again. She also had all the signs of someone with something to hide.

"I meant before that."

"The concert last night. He was so angry afterward. That's why we had the emergency rehearsal this morning."

"But you also saw him after the concert, didn't you?"

The young woman wilted, put her head in her hands and began sobbing. Pratt let her go on for a while.

"Miss Barna," he eventually asked, but kept his voice gentle, "would you please answer my question?"

She snuffled a moment longer, then raised her head and wiped her eyes and nose on her sleeves.

"You were seeing him, weren't you?"

She suddenly looked defiant. "Who told you? That Wanamaker woman, the orchestra's busybody?"

"So you're not denying it?"

"No. I suppose I can't. I know people in the orchestra guessed. I was careful. Luigi wasn't quite as careful. It wasn't his nature."

Pratt decided to take out his notebook. "Did you spend the night together?" At first he thought she wouldn't answer, but eventually he got a nod. "All night?"

"Do you also want a detailed description of what we did?" Sofia asked harshly.

"What was Spadafini's mood like?"

"He was very angry at the orchestra. He went on and on about it. Then just before midnight, his phone rang."

"His cell phone?"

"No. His home phone. I think he'd left his cell in the car. He got out of bed and took the call in his study. I heard a lot of shouting through the door."

"Do you know what the argument was about?"

"No. I think it was about money or something. The only clear thing I heard was about Luigi not owing anything."

"He used those exact words?"

She nodded.

"And did he say anything to you about it later?"

"Not a word. Actually, he was in a very good mood when he got back in bed. A very good mood…"

Sofia looked as if she was going to cry again. Pratt gave her some time to regain control.

"Did you come to this morning's rehearsal together?"

"Of course not! I took a cab from his place around nine o'clock and went home to change clothes."

"Then you came here."

She *just* kept from rolling her eyes. "We had a rehearsal."

"Did you speak to him at all after you left his apartment?"

"No."

"You had no communication whatso-ever? You didn't, for instance, go up to his office during the break?"

She looked really horrified. "Are you suggesting I murdered him?"

"I'm only trying to find out what happened. You were intimate with the man. It's a logical question."

"No! I didn't go to his office. Luigi was in a very bad mood. I stayed in the rehearsal room to practice. Ask anyone in the orchestra. I was there for the entire break."

"We will be asking."

"Everyone stayed either in the rehearsal room or the corridor outside. Some would have used the restrooms, I suppose. The break was only supposed to be a short one. We all stuck close by."

"No. One of you was up in Spadafini's office, strangling him."

Sofia Barna put her hand to her mouth and bolted from the stage.

CHAPTER EIGHT

P ratt stood in the doorway to the dead conductor's office again. In the hall behind him, the ambulance crew was waiting impatiently. It was nearly time to remove the body.

The Scene of Crime team had marked a number of things too small to see on the floor. With numbers beside each one, a team member was busy snapping photos. Two more were dusting the window frames for prints. The gray powder they used completely covered the desk. The team leader was crouched over the body watching the medical examiner do his thing.

Pratt called to the team leader, a man he knew well. "Frank, can you spare a minute?"

Frank Johnson walked to the doorway. "What can I do for you, Pratt?"

"How far have you gotten?"

Pratt braced himself. Johnson, known as a bit of a wiseass, liked to answer questions with song titles. He didn't disappoint.

"Well, I'll tell ya, it seems to be a case of 'Nothing from Nothing Leaves Nothing.' Whoever did the deed didn't leave much behind as far as we can see."

"No fingerprints?"

"Not many. Mr. Conductor Man over there seems to have been a bit of a neatnik. According to that guy Browne, the office would be cleaned at least once a day."

"Not many? I suppose you're going to have to fingerprint that whole crew in the basement, aren't you?"

Pratt sighed. "I suppose it will come to that. How about the body and the murder weapon?"

"We're not going to get anything out of the murder weapon, if I know my job. I found a few smudges consistent with gloves. Hard to tell what kind. We'll check for residue, but it will take time."

"And the body?"

"There's a bruise in the center of the guy's back consistent with somebody leaning on him with one knee and pulling back. That metal cable—"

"Cello string," Pratt added absently.

"Right. Your young assistant told us that's what it was. Anyway, the cello string dug into the guy's throat pretty deeply. A lot of bruising there."

Pratt and Johnson were joined by the medical examiner. "Death would have been pretty quick with that type of ligature," he told them as he peeled off his latex gloves.

"Just the amount of time it took the victim's lungs to run out of oxygen."

"And those drum mallets used to secure the ends of the cello string?" Pratt asked both of them.

The medico answered. "It would have been hard to hold a small cable like that really tight with bare or even gloved hands. Quite ingenious to use those sticks, actually. The murderer could make the length of the loop smaller so he could apply more pressure. If your arms are extended out like this"—the doctor held his arms far apart—"you can't put as much oomph behind it."

"Are you sure it was a male that did this?"

Both men looked doubtful to Pratt. Great. If they'd both come out strongly that they thought the murderer was male, it might have made things simpler.

"Hard to say," Johnson finally answered. "The stiff wasn't a very big guy. Good strong woman might have been able to do the deed."

"Doc?" Pratt asked, turning to him.

"I'll know more after the autopsy."

The usual answer from a medical examiner.

"Can you give me *anything* to work with?"

Both men looked at Pratt and then at each other.

Johnson said, "Well, there is one thing."

"What?"

"We found an open fountain pen on the desk. The nib was still wet, so it can't have been open that long."

"Can you give me a time."

"An hour only."

"And what was he writing?"

"Can't help you there. There was nothing on the desk, floor, wastebasket or on the body."

"Maybe he wrote on a pad?" the doctor threw in. "You might get impressions from the paper underneath."

Johnson shook his head and told him, "That only happens on TV."

"Gut reaction, Johnson," Pratt said, changing the subject. "Do you think you're going to find anything more useful here?"

Johnson sighed heavily. "No. This murderer was smart. So unless he or she was also extremely unlucky, no, we're not going to find anything. That's not to say we won't keep trying though."

Pratt nodded. "I appreciate that."

One of the other techs walked up. "We're ready to move the body now."

Pratt and the medical examiner stepped farther back in the hall to be out of the way.

"Will I see you at the autopsy?" he asked Pratt.

"Do you expect to find anything interesting?"

He shrugged. "Not really. But we always live in hope, don't we?"

Both men turned to watch the removal of the body.

"Detective Pratt, Detective Pratt!" Browne shouted as he appeared at the end of the hall. "I have to speak to you!"

The orchestra manager was coming fast. Behind him, looking much more relaxed, was Ellis. His face had a bit of a smirk.

Browne stopped right in front of Pratt, puffing like a bellows. "Your assistant has barred me from using my office! How can I do what you asked me to do if I can't use my office?"

Ellis shrugged. "I needed an Internet connection for my laptop."

"You can use the secretary's desk down the hall."

Pratt looked at Ellis, whose face was now studiously blank. What was the kid up to?

"We're all having to put up with a lot today," Pratt said.

"But I have things I must be doing—right now!"

"I'll make sure you can get back into your office ASAP. Okay?"

Browne looked as if he wanted to say something else, but Pratt returned his pointed glare. After a few seconds, Browne turned away and stomped off.

Pratt waited until he was well out of earshot before asking Ellis, "What was that all about?"

Now Ellis grinned. "Our friend Browne seemed a tad too eager to get into his office. He was the person who found the body, after all."

"I like the way you're thinking, my boy," Pratt said with a smirk of his own. "Now have you got anything else for me?"

"I went down to the rehearsal hall to look for you. Spadafini's overcoat was there, so I checked the pockets. His cell phone wasn't there, but in looking around, I found it on the floor. It appears to have been kicked under the conducting podium."

"I'm glad one of us is thinking," Pratt muttered under his breath.

"I checked his call history. There were several recent calls to a number on the other side of the country."

"And?"

"I did a reverse lookup of it. It's the phone number of the president of a rival orchestra—one that's currently looking for a new conductor."

CHAPTER NINE

This is unexpected, Pratt thought. "Did you call that number?" he asked Ellis.

"Naturally," the younger man answered. "My mother always says I was born curious. And what's more interesting, the phone number is for the chairman of the board's home phone number, not his office number."

"That's suggestive."

"I thought so too."

"So tell me about your phone call," Pratt said.

"The man himself answered on the first ring."

"What was his response when you told him what had happened?"

"He already knew. One of the other board members had just called him with the news," Ellis said.

"Lordy, that was quick."

"This is a really big deal. Spadafini was the hottest young conductor on the planet. And I checked out the street. You wouldn't believe the number of reporters and trucks out there."

Pratt could feel the pressure rising several more notches. "So did you learn anything else helpful?"

"I think you should get this information firsthand." Ellis handed over his cell phone. "I told him you'd call right away."

The detective had to admit he was impressed with Ellis. The lad could think on his feet—not that he'd say anything. The last thing a green detective needed was too much praise. That route led to a big head and sloppy work.

Pratt took the offered phone. It was already ringing. "This guy's name?"

"Julius Roseman."

The phone line clicked to life. "Hello?"

"Julius Roseman, please," Pratt said.

"This is he. Detective Pratt?"

"Yes. Would you be willing to answer some questions informally?"

"Certainly, although I have to say I'm still reeling from shock at what's happened. I spoke to Maestro Spadafini just this morning, quite early."

"May I ask what the conversation was about?"

"Well, there's no use hiding it now. It's all going to come out, I suppose. Spadafini was in talks with our orchestra's board to become our conductor."

Pratt opened his eyes wide at that news. Ellis flashed a quick smile and nodded.

"And does the management of his current orchestra know about this?"

"I know what you're thinking, Detective Pratt, but I assure you this is all above board. Although we've obviously had to be careful to keep everything under wraps."

"But did they know they were about to lose their star conductor?"

The phone was silent for a moment. "Spadafini was going to tell them," Roseman finally answered carefully. "He felt their offer of a bit more money was, shall we say, an insult to his current international standing. Our orchestra was prepared to pay him what he wanted. It's as simple as that."

"So he was going to jump ship."

"Well, you put it less delicately than I would, but yes. He was going to come to us."

Pratt frowned. "Was a contract signed?"

"My secretary was here preparing it. That is, until we got the news. Now, Detective Pratt, unless you have any more pressing questions, I have an emergency meeting of our board to attend. I'm sure you understand."

Pratt thought for a moment. "I will be asking your local police to come over and take a statement. They'll contact you to arrange a time. I'd also like to ask you to keep this information to yourself for the moment."

Roseman laughed. "Believe me, the last thing I want is our orchestra getting sucked into this mess."

"I won't keep you, then. Thank you for your help."

The line went dead. Obviously, Pratt had been dismissed by his better. He handed the cell phone back to Ellis.

"So what did he say?" Ellis asked.

Pratt normally would have resisted telling the youngster anything. After all, it wasn't as if they were partners. The older detective preferred working alone. This time, though, he felt thinking out loud might be of benefit, might help him order the facts in his mind, so he told Ellis.

"What's the next step?" the kid asked.

Pratt was about to answer when his walkie-talkie squawked. "Pratt," he answered simply.

It was the sergeant up at the stage entrance. "The chair of the symphony's board of directors is here. He's demanding to speak with you."

"Just what I need," the detective muttered to himself. "Tell him I'll be there in a moment." Pratt switched his walkie-talkie off and turned to Ellis. "I want you to dig around in Spadafini's past. See if you can find any more dirt."

"Got it," Ellis said and trotted off.

"Now, let's see what the big shot wants," Pratt said to himself with a heavy sigh as he headed for the stairs.

What he didn't need now was another person barking at him.

CHAPTER TEN

P ratt found a casually dressed gray-
haired man waiting by the security
desk. His foot tapped impatiently.

"Officer Pratt?"

"I am Detective Lieutenant Pratt," was
the curt reply.

"James Norris. I heard what the
sergeant here said to you, so you know
who I am. I demand to know what's going
on."

The best way to handle this joker
would be in private, Pratt knew. "Perhaps
we could talk in your office?"

Using the elevator, they arrived back upstairs at the opposite end of the corridor from Spadafini's office. Right in front of the elevator doors was a desk for a secretary. Pratt would have expected Browne to be there. Instead, they found the orchestra manager in his boss's office.

The boss was clearly not pleased.

"What are you doing in here, Browne?" Norris demanded.

"The police have thrown me out of my office and I need the use of a computer and the Internet."

"My secretary's desk is perfectly adequate for that."

Browne's face was carefully wiped of any emotion as he got to his feet. "I judged it would be better to work on the official press release in private."

"You judged wrongly. Now please leave. The detective is going to bring me up to speed on how his investigation is going."

Pratt caught the deep scowl on Browne's face as he shut the door.

"Tell me what you've found out about this tragedy," the president said as he took his seat behind the desk. He motioned the detective into another in front of it.

Pratt sized the man up for a moment. Clearly, he was used to people jumping on command. Maybe it would be good for Norris to jump for someone else for a change.

"I'd like to ask you a few questions first, if I may," Pratt began.

"I suppose that's understandable," was the answer as Norris leaned back in his chair. "All right. Ask away, Detective."

Pratt flipped open his notebook. "Give me your impressions of Spadafini."

"Let's see...A musical genius, absolutely brilliant. Hardworking. Difficult at times. The man knew what he wanted and wouldn't take second best for anything.

The orchestra has really flourished under him."

"Even though they didn't like him?"

"Yes, I suppose that has to be taken into account. As I said, he wouldn't take anything but the best—especially in performance. Confidentially, the board encouraged him to get rid of the deadwood. We had a lot of musicians who were well past their best-before date."

"Would that include the two musicians who died last year?"

Norris looked up sharply. "Not so much with the Lee woman, but that timpani player certainly needed replacing."

"And hounding someone is an appropriate way to get rid of them?"

"The orchestra has a pretty ironclad contract. It's something our current board would like to get better control of. Presenting classical music is a very costly undertaking. We want only the best."

"What was your personal relationship with Spadafini like?"

"Cordial and professional. Occasionally, I'd be forced to step in when he went a bit overboard. The man had very little sense about what things actually cost."

"There was no, ah, friction?"

"Not really. No."

Pratt tapped his pencil against his notebook for a moment. "I understand his contract was coming up for renewal. How was that going?"

"Very well. Due to Spadafini, our ticket sales have been much stronger, especially since he's had a bestselling CD—with our orchestra on it."

Norris looked away as he answered, and Pratt was certain he was lying.

"So you're confident that you would have re-signed him?"

"That was the board's feeling, yes."

Again a lie. "Would it surprise you then to find out that he'd been talking to another orchestra and had in fact agreed to jump ship?"

Bingo! A direct hit on that. Norris's face turned a heavy crimson.

"Who told you that?"

"The chairman of the other orchestra. Spadafini spoke to him as recently as this morning, minutes before he was murdered, I might add."

"How did you find that out?"

"I'm not at liberty to say. And you knew nothing about this?"

"Spadafini made the intimation that he would leave if we didn't meet his price. Frankly, I thought it was just a ploy to get more money out of us."

Pratt mentally crossed his fingers with the next question. He really needed it answered. "And the contract renegotiations, how was this handled?"

"Spadafini had no manager. He didn't trust them. I, of course, represented the board."

"Would you have matched the offer this new orchestra made?"

"Detective, how can I answer that without knowing the dollar amount?"

"You would have let him go, then, if you felt it was too high?"

Norris hesitated a moment before saying, "Of course, we would have tried to retain his services! But we have to keep our bottom line in sight too. We owe that to our community." Norris sat up straight and leaned forward. "But this is all beside the point now that he's dead, isn't it?"

"Perhaps."

"Now could you please tell me what progress you've made on discovering who murdered our conductor?"

Pratt was about to answer when his walkie-talkie squawked again.

Two people were trying to talk to him at once.

One was the detective he'd left in charge on the interview detail with the orchestra. "You'd better come down here. We've got something interesting."

The other was Ellis. "Where are you? I've got some things you need to know."

"Pratt here. Both of you meet me in the hallway outside the rehearsal room." Then the detective turned to Norris. "Sorry, sir, but as you can see, there are developments. Will you be around later?"

"Possibly."

"I'll catch up with you then."

As Pratt hustled for the elevator, he thought about the three times he was certain Norris had lied to him. Experience told him that people most normally looked away when they were lying. The only decorative thing on Norris's desk was a framed photo of a beautiful young woman.

A daughter, perhaps, or maybe a second wife? Each time the man had lied to Pratt, he'd looked at that photo. The last time had been the longest. It had followed Pratt's question about Spadafini leaving the orchestra.

The detective was pretty sure Norris didn't want the horny conductor anywhere near that woman.

CHAPTER ELEVEN

Food was being delivered into the rehearsal room when Pratt arrived at its doors. He looked longingly at the boxes. All he'd had that morning was a cup of dispenser coffee. Still, a missed meal would cut down on the gut he'd developed since Dori walked out on their marriage. A diet of fast food will do that to you.

"What do you have for me, Cooper?" he asked the detective who'd called him.

"We found something in the instrument storage lockers."

The room next door had lockers where the orchestra's musicians could securely store their instruments if they didn't want to take them home. The detective explained that they also used the lockers to store various odds and ends they might need, along with purses and the like.

"I hit on the idea of asking each musician we questioned to open their lockers for us before we talked. I thought maybe our murderer might have stashed something here."

Two lockers were open as they entered the long, narrow room. One was large and on the bottom row. They went to that first.

Pratt asked, "Whose locker?"

"A trombone player."

But there was a cello inside. Pratt crouched to look at it. The second-thickest string was missing.

"You said the stiff upstairs had been choked by a string from one of these."

Pratt got to his feet. "So how did the trombonist explain this?"

"He claims it's not his instrument. He's only keeping it in here as a favor for someone else."

"Whose cello is it?"

The detective flipped his notebook back a page. "An orchestra member who died last year."

Pratt felt his heart beat faster. "Annabelle Lee?"

"You know about that?"

"Why does this guy have her cello?" Pratt shot back.

"Like I said: someone in the orchestra asked him to keep it in here."

"Who?"

The detective consulted his notes. "Someone named Daniel Harvey."

"Have you spoken to him?"

"Not yet. That's why I called you."

Pratt's mind was racing. He felt like a bloodhound that had suddenly picked up the scent. A real smile split his face for the first time that day.

He pointed to the other open locker farther down the room. "What about that?"

"That belongs to one of the percussionists."

"Let me guess: he's missing a pair of his sticks."

The other detective grinned. "Got it in one. Special ones too."

Pratt already had his walkie-talkie out. "Johnson! You still here?"

It took nearly twenty seconds, but the walkie-talkie eventually crackled and the Scene of Crime tech's voice said clearly, "Yeah. We're still working over the room."

"The evidence bag with the murder weapon, is that still here?"

"Yeah."

"I'm going to send someone up for it, okay?"

"Just make sure I get it back promptly."

"Sure, sure. I also need someone down here to work over the instrument storage room. There's some evidence that needs collecting." Pratt turned back to the detective with him. "Get one of the uniforms to go up two floors to the offices and fetch an evidence bag. In the meantime, bring that Harvey character in here. I want to hear what he has to say."

While the detective was out of the room, Pratt found Ellis via the walkie-talkie. "So what do you need to tell me?" he asked.

"Well, based on stuff I found on news sites on the Internet, our boy seems to have been a regular Don Juan. The ladies all seemed to go gaga over him. There's a fan page on Facebook, for pity's sake. Anyway, he lost a chance at conducting one of the big European orchestras because of his habits with the females."

"Anything else?"

"There's not a peep anywhere about Spadafini possibly jumping ship."

"I need you to do something else for me. Find out what phone numbers belong to James Norris. I—"

"The chairman of the orchestra's board?" Ellis interrupted.

Pratt shouldn't have been surprised that the kid knew. He was proving to be pretty sharp.

"Yes. Get his home and cell phone numbers, then cross-check it with any numbers that Spadafini has called recently."

"I'll also check his text messages. I may have missed something when I glanced at it earlier. Most of what is there is soft-core porn chatter with his current girlfriend."

"That little thing? She seemed so darn innocent when I was talking to her earlier."

"They're the worst ones." Ellis laughed.

"Whatever. Find me what I want and then meet me down here. We're finally making some progress—I hope."

"Right. I'll be down ASAP."

A tall, slender man with graying hair appeared·in the doorway. Pratt looked at him for a long moment just to make the musician a bit more apprehensive. Satisfyingly, he glanced twice at the open locker.

"Are you Daniel Harvey?" Pratt asked.

"Yes. Yes, I am."

"Could I ask you to look at something for me?"

The man licked his lips nervously. "Of course. I'm happy to assist the police."

He doesn't look it, Pratt thought. "That's good. Step this way please."

Pratt led Harvey to the locker where the cello was. They both crouched down.

"Can you identify this instrument?" he asked.

Harvey started to reach for it, and Pratt grabbed his arm.

"Don't touch that, sir. It's evidence in our murder investigation."

Perhaps that was laying it on a bit thick, but Pratt felt making the musician nervous would get the best—and quickest—results.

"It's, ah, it's..." Harvey was struggling to keep himself together. "It belonged to Annabelle Lee, who used to play in this orchestra."

"I know. She committed suicide last year."

"Yes. Yes, she did."

"And why do you have her cello?"

Harvey looked at Pratt with very frightened eyes.

"She was my cousin."

CHAPTER TWELVE

Without a word, Pratt stood, and the musician collapsed to his knees.

"I did not kill Spadafini! You have to believe me. Much as I wanted to, I didn't do it!"

"I'd like to believe that."

"You have to. I...I was with someone during the entire break. I didn't leave this floor."

"Who?" the detective asked.

"Leanne Shapiro. I was with her the entire time. Other people saw me too."

Now they had something to run with.
"Ellis!" he barked into the walkie-talkie.
"Where are you?"

"On my way down the stairs. What's
happening?"

"Just double-time it, okay? I need you."

Pratt walked over to Detective Cooper,
who was standing in the doorway, and said
in low voice, "This Shapiro woman, if she's
already been questioned, find out what she
said. If she hasn't, do it now. Don't tell her
anything about what's going down. Maybe,
just maybe, we've gotten lucky."

"Got it." The detective angled his head.
"What about this guy?"

"Move him to an empty room. I think
I'll let Ellis have a shot at him."

Ellis arrived, breathless and looking
eager. "I've got some news."

"Not now. Things are moving a bit fast
at the moment."

"There's a break?"

Pratt couldn't help smiling. "I hope so. It's too soon to know." He filled the young man in on what had been happening. "You question Harvey more thoroughly. I didn't have time to go into why he has his cousin's cello. It may have something to do with the case, it may not, but we need to know."

Ellis hustled Harvey out. Pratt closed the door and leaned against it to catch his breath—and think.

In his twenty-eight years as a detective, he'd never had a case like this. In one way, it was a dream. Unless there was something he was missing completely, the murderer was still here. Any evidence was still here.

The silliness of the orchestra's mass-confession aside, the big problem was that any one of them could have done it. That meant questioning a really huge pool of suspects.

Spadafini had obviously been a bastard of the first water. His womanizing alone was outrageous, but his treatment of the people he worked with was contemptible. Pratt felt sure that was the reason for his death.

So, who did it? Pratt was looking for a crowbar, that bit of information he could use to pry the truth loose. The real issue was being able to pick out the important clues from the mass of information they were collecting.

His biggest enemy was time. All these people couldn't be kept here forever. Getting them fed and watered was only buying him a bit more time. Would the murderer give it up under questioning? He doubted it. For the moment he or she could hide in plain sight.

The tired detective shook his head. And that indeed was the problem: how to smoke out the murderer.

Pulling out his cell phone, he dialed the captain.

"Pratt! What have you got for me?"

The situation was quickly outlined.

"I could really use more people," Pratt told his boss. "We're stretched too thin, and time is running out. I can't keep the orchestra here forever."

"I'll have to shake someone else's tree. You've got everyone from here." The captain changed the subject. "Did you talk to *El Presidente* of the symphony's board?"

"Yeah, Norris was here. He may still be around, as a matter of fact. He wanted an update on where we stood. I got called away."

"Not a nice man to cross, I would think. When I got called up to the chief's office, he was there with the mayor to turn up the heat on us." The captain chuckled. "I probably shouldn't tell you this, but Norris said he was going to go down there to personally shake things up. On his way out he was grumbling that it was his second trip down of the day and he had better—"

"What did you say? Pratt interrupted. "He was here already this morning? When?"

"Norris said he'd had to come down to thank the orchestra for coming in for the extra rehearsal. He talked about what a sensitive bunch they are, how they needed to be stroked all the time. Didn't he tell you about that?"

"No, he didn't," Pratt growled. "And I'm going to find out why."

CHAPTER THIRTEEN

P ratt took the stairs back up two at a time. His tiredness was forgotten. He hated being played by someone.

He found Norris in his office with Browne. Both men looked up in surprise at the abrupt entry.

"Why didn't you tell me you'd already been down here this morning?" Pratt asked angrily.

"Look here, Detective! I don't like your tone."

"I don't like people not being honest with me."

"In case you don't remember our earlier conversation, you never asked me."

"Well, I'm asking now." Pratt sat on the other vacant seat in front of the desk and made a show of taking out his notebook and pen. "When were you down here and why?"

"I don't have to talk to you."

The detective got to his feet again. "Okay. Play it that way. We'll talk downtown. Bring a whole law firm to hold your hand if you want. I don't care. But just remember that you're going to be escorted out of here in front of all those reporters outside."

Pratt pulled out his walkie-talkie and turned up the volume again.

After looking at Browne for a moment, Norris got to his feet too. "Perhaps I spoke hastily, Detective. Please...take a seat."

Knowing he had to keep the upper hand, Pratt nodded, then sat. "Tell me about this morning."

"Our concert last night wasn't the best, at least in Spadafini's eyes. The man was a bloody perfectionist. Tonight's performance was going to be recorded for a radio broadcast, so he demanded an extra rehearsal. To keep him happy, I agreed. Of course, our musicians were furious, so it was up to me to placate them with a little pep talk before the rehearsal."

"What time was that?"

"Nine o'clock. I spoke for about five minutes and promised them all a bit of a bonus as a token of thanks from the board. I departed immediately afterward."

"Where did you go?"

"Directly home."

In order to build up a little tension, Pratt made a show of looking back at several pages in his notebook. "You and the mayor were in the chief's office before the press even got wind of what happened down here. How did you find—"

"From me," Browne interrupted. "I called Mr. Norris right after my call to the police."

Pratt turned to the orchestra manager. "Who else did you call?"

"Um...my wife to tell her I certainly wouldn't be home for lunch."

"Oh really."

"And where did you call Mr. Norris from?"

"I used my cell phone. As chairman of the board, he needed to know right away."

"Your cell phone."

"Yes."

"Detective Pratt," Norris said, "I appreciated that Browne was doing such a good job under very trying circumstances. I'm not sure I would have thought of something like that if I had been in his place. We're very lucky to have Mr. Browne."

Pratt brought his attention back to Norris. "When you left, did anyone see you?"

"The security guard was at his desk, if that's what you mean."

"I was with him too," Browne added.

Pratt looked at Norris, again with a pause. "And you went right home."

Norris returned the stare. "I went right home."

"At home, who saw you?"

"My daughter and her boyfriend."

"Anyone else?"

"I wasn't home long. Maybe our maid. I really don't remember."

Seeing that there wasn't much more to be gained, Pratt got to his feet. "I see you're working on a press release," he said, looking down at a sheet of paper on Norris's desk.

"We have to say something. The longer we wait, the worse it will be."

"I have to ask you not to release this until I've taken a look at it. I'm sure you wouldn't want to compromise the investigation."

"No. Of course not. Speaking of which, are you any closer to knowing what happened?"

"We've found out a number of useful things. I have hopes."

Pratt left them and walked down the hall a short distance. Outside Browne's office, a uniformed cop was standing.

"Any problems with the locals?" Pratt asked.

"If you mean Browne, how about every ten minutes or so? Are you keeping him out of his office just to annoy him?"

"Maybe."

The cop smiled. "Good. He's a jackass."

Pratt's walkie-talkie had been turned off for nearly ten minutes, and as he took the elevator down one floor to the security desk, he listened to the wash of chatter. Seemed as if everyone wanted to talk to him.

"I'm at the security desk," Pratt was saying as the elevator doors opened. "Sorry for being offline. Ellis—you there?"

Through a bit of crackle, Ellis said, "Live and in person."

"Good. Do you know where the Green Room is?"

"I'm sitting in it right now."

"Sit tight. I'll be there shortly."

The security guard was standing just inside the stage door, talking to the two cops guarding it.

Pratt motioned him over to his desk. "You were on all morning?"

"I came on duty at seven AM."

"James Norris, do you know him by sight?"

The guard snorted. "Of course. Been working here five years, haven't I?"

"Did you see him arrive this morning?"

"I buzzed him in shortly before the orchestra started rehearsing."

"When did he leave?"

"About fifteen minutes later. I let him out."

"But he has a key.

"I suppose so. I've never seen him use it."

"So he could have come back in again."

"Why?"

Pratt wanted to throttle the man. "Let's just say he did, okay?"

"Well, I've been here all morning, but I did my rounds starting at ten-oh-five and was gone for twelve, maybe fifteen minutes. I suppose he could have come back in." The guard looked down at his cubicle. "But we'd have a video record of it, wouldn't we?"

"Did the sergeant who was up here look through the security recordings?"

The guard nodded once.

"Did he look at the footage showing the stage door?"

Again the single nod. "I helped him."

"And what did it show?"

"Nothing. The camera ain't been working for a week. I've called in for a repairman and complained to Browne."

Pratt heaved a sigh as he headed down the hall to the Green Room.

When he got there, Ellis was sitting on a sofa, legs crossed, while he scribbled madly in his notebook.

"What can I do for you, sir?" he asked when he looked up.

Pratt sat down heavily at the other end of the sofa, not bothering to correct him.

"Get anything interesting out of Harvey?"

"No. He has his cousin's cello to keep it safe. She didn't have a will, and her mother and father are fighting over it. I had no idea the darn things were that expensive!"

"What about his alibi?"

Ellis nodded and checked a page in his notebook. "Harvey was actually in full view of three other orchestra members for the entire break. We checked with each separately and they all had the same story. Here's a theory. Do you think he may have had something to do with it? Maybe there were several people in on the murder. He supplied the cello string, someone else the timpani mallets and a third person did the deed. What do you think?"

"I suppose it could be something like that, but…I don't think so."

"You have some thoughts on how this thing went down?"

"I don't want to lead you down the garden path."

"What do you mean?"

"Being a good detective means sifting through a lot of evidence. It means keeping your eyes and mind open at all times. It means leaving no stone unturned. Do that, catch a little bit of luck, and you should get to the truth."

"I know that."

"You seem like a bright kid. I don't want you getting wrong ideas on how this game is played."

Ellis looked puzzled. "Sir?"

Pratt debated for a moment. This kid needed to go through the school of hard knocks if he had any hope of becoming a good detective. Acting on hunches was not part of that. It was risky, and you often wound up with egg on your face—or worse. This wasn't the time to play fast and loose. Or was it? Everything about this case was out of the ordinary.

"Kid...sometimes, not always, you have to play a hunch, go with what you feel in your gut. Today might be one of those days."

Unexpectedly, Ellis grinned. "I was hoping you'd say something like that."

"Huh?"

"For the past half hour, I've been following up a hunch and uncovered some interesting information. I've been hesitant to tell you. They all say you play by the book."

Pratt came to a decision. "Tell me what you've been thinking, and then I'll do likewise."

It surprised Pratt that Ellis had come to the same conclusions, but from a totally different starting point. Ellis had used technology. Pratt's was based on observation and deduction.

"The only thing now is that we have to prove it or get the person to admit it," Pratt said.

"I may be able to help there. Like I said, I've been doing some extra digging. I had to break a few rules though."

Pratt's expression tightened. "Meaning?"

"I, ah…Some of the information I got should have been accompanied by a search warrant."

Ellis quickly sketched out what that information was.

"That's always the sticking point in this racket. We'll hold that information back and get the search warrants later." Oddly, though, Pratt felt much better, more certain they were on the right track. "Now, here's what I want you to do—and no improvising!"

They talked for a few more minutes, during which Ellis scribbled notes, nodding his understanding.

At the end, Pratt clapped Ellis on the shoulder. "Well, kid, either we're going to kick this one through the goalposts—"

"Or they're going to kick us to the street."

"Something like that."

CHAPTER FOURTEEN

P ratt walked into the rehearsal room with Ellis. The orchestra was still eating, and the smells of the sandwiches and salads made his stomach rumble. Everyone looked up at them with unfriendly eyes.

Eliza Wanamaker wasn't hard to spot. She was surrounded by other musicians. It looked like a meeting.

Pratt walked over. "I'd like to speak with you again."

"Is this about letting us get the hell out of here sometime soon?"

The musicians around her nodded their agreement.

"I'm afraid not. I have some more questions."

She got to her feet. "I suppose you want to do this in private?"

"That was the idea."

As they left the room, Pratt could see Ellis in a far corner speaking with Sofia Barna, the piccolo player who'd spent the previous night with Spadafini.

Both had their questions to ask, and hopefully, they'd get the answers they needed.

Twenty minutes later, Ellis and Pratt met to share the information the two women had given them.

Pratt said, "Now it just remains to talk to Mr. Browne and see what he has to say."

"I'm ready," Ellis said with a nod.

"No, you're not. I want you to call the captain and tell him that we want those search warrants—and to step on it. Are you clear on everything?"

The young detective nodded.

"Good. You'll find me with Browne in his office when you're done."

Ellis grinned. "He'll be thrilled to see me."

"No doubt."

Pratt found the orchestra manager still with his boss. Neither of them looked happy.

"Any news, Detective?" both of them asked.

"We've made some progress on the huge list of suspects," Pratt answered. "Mr. Browne, I take it you're the person most familiar with the members of the orchestra?"

Browne nodded. "I should hope so."

"Great. I need to discuss some of them with you. It will help greatly in getting us closer to the answers we're all looking for. Maybe we could use your office to talk?"

Behind his desk, Norris's face brightened. "Does that mean I might finally be able to go home?"

"Could you stay around just a little bit longer? I've asked one of my detectives to come in and take your statement, go over a few things. Is that all right?"

"I suppose it will have to do."

The uniformed cop stationed outside Browne's office was gone. Browne and Pratt went inside and made themselves comfortable. On the desk, beside a computer monitor and the phone, was a photo of a rather plain woman and two children, a boy and a girl who looked to be in their early teens.

"Nice-looking family," Pratt said.

"Thanks." Browne rested his arms on the desk and leaned forward confidently. "Now, what can I do for you, Detective Pratt?"

"You told me earlier you don't have much day-to-day contact with members of the orchestra."

"I said I don't have time to attend most rehearsals. I am a very busy man. This organization would grind to a halt without me. Of course I had to make sure everyone knew the schedule for rehearsals and concerts. I had to—"

Pratt held up his hand. "Suffice it to say, though, that if anyone knew what was going on with the orchestra's musicians, it would likely be you."

Browne smiled. "Of course. It's part of my job."

"Obviously, you were also in daily contact with Spadafini."

"When he was in town, yes."

"So it's safe to assume that you would have been aware of the goings-on between him and some of the orchestra's female members."

"If you're referring to Annabelle Lee, I had no idea that anything was going on until she took her own life."

"That's not what I've been told."

CHAPTER FIFTEEN

The expression on the orchestra manager's face was confused. Then he flushed angrily as the comment sank in.

"What exactly are you trying to say, Detective?"

Pratt pretended to soothe him. "It's natural that you would want to protect the organization's most valuable asset. Keeping things running smoothly is part of your job, isn't it? And so is loyalty."

Browne leaned back in his chair. "I suppose I wasn't completely forthright with you at the beginning, and for that

I apologize." He sighed heavily. "Sometimes I feel like the father confessor around here. I have to listen to the board's complaints, the conductor's, the soloists', the guest conductors', and always the musicians'. It gets pretty wearing. Everybody expects me to sort out their problems."

"I understand completely. So what exactly did you know about Spadafini's, ah, indiscretions?"

"Well…pretty much everything. A number of people in the orchestra, older women actually, complained about Spadafini's carrying-on almost from the moment he arrived. I think they were bitter they couldn't attract his attention, if you want to know the truth."

Pratt chuckled. "I think I've met one of them."

"Eliza Wanamaker?" When Pratt nodded, Browne added, "Damn woman thinks she's the conscience of the orchestra."

Someone knocked softly on the office door.

It was Ellis, as planned. "Sir, you wanted to see me?"

Pratt turned. "Yes. You take notes faster than I can, so come in here and take notes."

Ellis sat on one of the chairs around a low table in a corner of the office, an informal meeting area. Crossing his legs, he pulled out his notebook. Pratt hoped he would play his part well.

The older detective continued, "So Spadafini confided in you?"

Browne noticeably swelled. "All the time." Then he pursed his lips. "Luigi also constantly asked me to help clean up his little messes, as he called them."

"Such as?"

Michael Browne considered for a moment. "I suppose it doesn't make any difference now...Annabelle Lee gave me a letter to pass on to the orchestra's board.

It was after the last rehearsal she attended. She knew there was a board meeting the next day. On her way home, she jumped in front of the subway train." He sighed. "I'm afraid I opened that letter. I, ah, never gave it to the board."

Pratt leaned forward to speak. "What happened to it?"

"I gave it to Luigi and he tore it to shreds. Wouldn't even look at it."

"Just like the letter you told me she sent to him."

Browne nodded. "Looking back, I guess it's not my proudest moment."

"What did it say?"

"She went on and on about how he'd seduced her, almost raped her after he took her out to dinner the first time. How he'd lied about his feelings for her. I don't know if any of that was actually true, but she was obviously a very naive and hurt young woman. But what she was saying could have been very damaging for the orchestra."

"Did she ever accompany Spadafini to a public function?"

"What?" A smile came over his face. "Oh, I see where you're going with that. No. Everyone in the orchestra knew they were involved, just like that silly piccolo player he was boinking recently. There were a number of others in and out of the orchestra too, soloists, even an usher. Let's just say he was an alpha male."

"So you covered for Luïgi Spadafini, smoothed the way for him over rough waters."

Browne looked suddenly wary. "My job is to help make this orchestra run smoothly. Public scandals involving our conductor would not have been good for the orchestra. I did nothing illegal."

"How would you describe your relationship with Spadafini?"

"Cordial. I got along with him better than most."

"And he relied on you."

The orchestra manager nodded. "I helped him a lot."

"What did you get out of it?"

"The satisfaction of a job well done," Browne replied almost smugly.

"Somehow I think that there was more to it than that." Pratt turned to the younger detective in the corner. "Ellis, were you able to get more information about what we were talking about earlier?"

"Certainly."

"And could you tell Mr. Browne about it? We don't need the exact words. Just sum it up."

Ellis consulted his notebook (for show), then cleared his throat. "At twelve eighteen, I was in the orchestra's rehearsal hall and noticed a cell phone on the floor partially under the conductor's podium.

Further examination showed that it belonged to Luigi Spadafini. It must have fallen from the pocket of his overcoat. On its call history was a record of a dozen phone calls to Mr. Browne's cell over the past two weeks. I also found a number of incoming calls, all from Mr. Browne's cell phone, as—"

"How can you possibly find that suspicious?" Browne interrupted. "We were consulting about next season's programming."

"Why would you be using a cell phone at all?" Pratt asked. "Some of those calls came in the middle of the day when you were both here. We've checked. Why wouldn't you just stroll down the hall to talk to him? If you were both that lazy, you could have used your office phones. Why talk on a cell every time? That's what made us suspicious."

"I don't know. I'm just so used to using my cell, I suppose. I reach for that first, that's all. Luigi too."

"Really?"

"Yes, goddammit!"

Ellis got up and handed a scrap of paper to Pratt, who pushed it across the desk toward Browne.

"Recognize that phone number?"

"No. Should I?" Browne's forehead now had a light sheen of sweat.

"We also found that number in the call history of Spadafini's cell phone. Being curious, we dialed it. The person at the other end told us some very interesting things. Luigi Spadafini was planning on jumping ship. You agreed with my statement that he relied on you. Surely you knew about this."

Browne looked at his watch. "James Norris told me about this not half an hour ago. It came as a very great shock. Luigi never said a word about it."

"I'll come back to this. Just before I came up here, I spoke with Eliza Wanamaker. I was curious as to why you told the orchestra about the murder. I think you told me you just blurted it out."

"That's correct. I was very upset."

"Funny. Eliza got the feeling that you didn't seem at all upset. She described you as outwardly calm and in control."

"Appearances can be deceiving, Detective. Surely I shouldn't have to tell you that."

"Why then did you pick up Spadafini's overcoat before you left the room? Ms. Wanamaker remembers that clearly. Everyone was in a panic, and you caused that. Were you trying to distract them so you could search for Spadafini's cell phone?"

Now Browne was definitely sweating.

Pratt continued. "I think you wanted it to disappear along with the record of all those calls."

"That's a lie!" Browne shouted.

Pratt was about to hammer another nail into the coffin when the office door opened. Norris stuck his head in, and Browne used the interruption to leap to his feet.

"James! How fortunate you've shown up. The detectives here seem to want to drag me into this mess. Please come in. I want a witness to hear the outrageous accusations."

Browne came around the desk and opened the door wide. Grabbing his boss by the arm, he whipped him into the room, directly where Pratt was seated. The two men collided hard, knocking over Pratt's chair. In a flash, Browne was through the doorway. Equally fast, Ellis jumped right over the low table in front of him and disappeared out the door.

As he struggled to get up, Pratt heard a loud cry followed by a crash. By the time he got out to the hall, it was all over. The orchestra manager lay on his stomach with the youthful Ellis on top of him.

"Get off me! Get him off me!" Browne shouted.

Ellis grinned up at Pratt. "You wouldn't happen to have any handcuffs, would you?"

He did. Handcuffs were his good luck charm and he always had his pair in a jacket pocket. Ellis placed them around the orchestra manager's wrists with a satisfying *click*. They pulled Browne to his feet.

"Why did you do it?" Pratt asked calmly.

"Because Spadafini was a complete bastard! He deserved to die. When he told me he wasn't taking me to the new orchestra, he laughed! I wasn't going to let him screw me just like he screwed everyone else."

As they led their prisoner to the elevator, Pratt said with a laugh, "Let me guess, Ellis. You were also a star on your high school track team. Hurdles, right?"

The young detective nodded. "Got it in one, sir...I mean, Pratt."

CHAPTER SIXTEEN

All the six o'clock news showed was someone being led out the stage door, an overcoat pulled up over his head. There were a lot of loose ends to tie up, so all Pratt would say to the crowd of reporters was that someone had been arrested for the murder of Luigi Spadafini. There would be a news conference the next morning.

As the film clip played on the TV in the corner of the captain's office, Pratt, Ellis and McDonnell were watching it carefully.

"Pretty slick bit of detecting, Pratt," the captain laughed. He'd enjoyed telling the chief and mayor that the crisis was over.

"It's because our young Detective Ellis is a nosy bastard with good instincts. He's also a dab hand with a computer—and fast on his feet."

The captain leaned back in his chair. "Tell me about it, Ellis."

"It actually was lucky that I decided to use Browne's office because that gave me access to his computer. I only needed his connection to the Internet for my laptop. I did happen to turn on his computer, though, since I was there. It had a password, but I figured that out on the first try. It was his wife's name, and that was on the family photo on his desk. Amazing how many people do something that simple."

When the captain started to say something, Pratt held up his hand.

"The lad knows how illegal that was. But it got us some important information. With that warrant they're hopefully getting signed now, we can 'officially' find the information Ellis uncovered. It will make our case even stronger."

"Which was?"

"Browne kept copious notes. There's a ledger, I guess you could call it, that tracks who he helped, why and what he expected to get out of it. Spadafini had promised to take him to the new orchestra and become its manager. It was supposed to be payback for all the crap Browne had shoveled for him. Unfortunately, the conductor was a lying bastard. Last night he told Browne he'd never even told the other orchestra about their deal—and he wasn't going to. The girl Spadafini was with last night heard one end of that argument. When we arrested Browne, he had his cell phone in his pocket. Since it was now evidence, we checked.

Sure enough, in its history there was a phone call to Spadafini at precisely that time."

"I interviewed the girl a second time," Ellis added. "And she'd heard more than she'd told Pratt originally. She thought from what she heard that it was an orchestra member on the phone. After the murder, she didn't want to rat on any of her colleagues. She didn't think that would go down well."

"Nice girl," McDonnell said. "And getting lied to about a new job was enough to push Browne over the edge?"

Pratt let Ellis answer again.

"Seems as if Browne had done more than cover up Spadafini's indiscretions. There were some illegal things."

"Like what?"

"We're not sure yet. He alluded to something involving an underage girl. About that time, a lawyer showed up and turned off the tap. We'll get it out of him somehow."

The captain shook his head. "So why did the orchestra pull that 'we're all guilty' stunt?"

Pratt answered. "Because they were all convinced that one of them had done it. It worked perfectly for Browne. He'd known all the scuttlebutt going down among them, how they'd been jokingly coming up with ways to kill their conductor. This morning he just gave it a little push."

"If Browne had recovered Spadafini's cell phone after the murder," Ellis added, "he only needed to lose it. We might never have thought to check the phone company's records and connect up the dots. Browne might actually have gotten away with it."

The captain shook his head again. "Maybe you won't complain about cell phones anymore, eh, Pratt? One of them saved your sorry ass today." McDonnell got to his feet. "Good job, both of you. Now I'm going home to persuade my wife she isn't mad at me for being down here on my day off."

The two detectives were headed for home too.

As they stopped to get their coats, Ellis turned to Pratt. "You said earlier that you'd heard Spadafini conduct several times. What was he like as a musician?"

"Incredible. He could make you hear a piece of music as if it was the first time. I don't think I've ever been to more exciting concerts."

"And he was such a…well, a scumbag as a person."

"Yeah, kid. Welcome to our world. You'll find when you dig below the surface, a lot of people are pretty ugly. In my experience, the more ability a person has, the greater the ugliness."

Ellis held out his hand to Pratt. "Thank you for letting me work with you today— and for trusting me."

"Thank the captain. He dumped you on me. Remember?" Then Pratt clapped Ellis on the shoulder. "How about if we go out for a couple of beers and a good steak dinner with all the trimmings? My treat. Got anything on?"

"I'm in—just as long as the restaurant's background music isn't classical."

ACKNOWLEDGMENTS

The author would like to thank Vicki Blechta and Cheryl Freedman for their help in reviewing the manuscript for this book, and for their useful comments—and corrections. He would also like to thank Jill Kirwan for conversations past, present and future about all things orchestral. Thanks must also go to Bob Tyrrell and his staff for their help in bringing this book to print.

RICK BLECHTA has two passions in life: music and writing. A professional musician since age fourteen, he brings his extensive knowledge of that life to his crime fiction. He is now the author of six novels, one of which, *Cemetery of the Nameless*, was shortlisted for the Arthur Ellis Best Novel Award (2005).